MUMMY MAYHEM

Steve Barlow and Steve Skidmore

Illustrated by Alex Lopez

EDGE · FRANKLIN WATTS

LONDON·SYDNEY

Franklin Watts
First published in Great Britain in 2017 by The Watts Publishing Group

Credits
Executive Editor: Adrian Cole
Design Manager: Peter Scoulding
Cover Designer: Cathryn Gilbert
Illustrations: Alex Lopez

HB ISBN 978 1 4451 5376 6
PB ISBN 978 1 4451 5378 0
Library ebook ISBN 978 1 4451 5377 3

Printed in China.

MIX
Paper from
responsible sources
FSC
www.fsc.org FSC® C104740

Franklin Watts
An imprint of
Hachette Children's Group
Part of The Watts Publishing Group
Carmelite House
50 Victoria Embankment
London EC4Y 0DZ

An Hachette UK Company
www.hachette.co.uk

www.franklinwatts.co.uk

Lin

Danny

Sam

"You can read this?" asked Lin.

Danny nodded. "Sure. Demons know how to read old writing."

"So what does it say?"

"It says, 'Don't mess with my coffin.
Or you'll be in big trouble. Best wishes,
King Tut'."

Lin gasped. "The mummy's curse!
But what does it mean? 'Don't mess
with the coffin'?"

"I think so," said Danny. "Look.
The mummies will return to their coffins.
But only if Anubis tells them."
Sam pointed at Lin. "Turn into a
werewolf. You can pretend to be Anubis!"

"You'll be fine," said Sam.

"Lead the mummies back to their coffins," said Danny. "Sam and I will do the rest."

"Did you see anything odd?"
asked Mr Broad.
"No, sir," said Danny,
Lin and Sam.

"Let's get out of here!"

Clogger moaned.